Dear Parent:

Here is a story about a special friendship. Duck and Bear both have unique personalities. But it doesn't stop them from being great friends. All it requires is mutual acceptance of their differences.

Reading *Two Good Friends* might provide some opportunities to discuss what makes a good friend, and how to be a good friend. It could also be a good opportunity to talk about being tidy: who wants to get stuck in honey, anyway!

This is an early book by two individuals who have since made a name for themselves in children's books. Giulio Maestro, together with his wife Betsy, has created some award-winning nonfiction picture books for children, including *The Story of the Statue of Liberty*. Judy Delton has written a number of bestselling books for older children and is probably best known for her *Pee Wee Scouts* series.

We hope that Duck and Bear become favorite friends at your house.

Sincerely,

Stephen Fraser

Stephen Fraser
Senior Editor
Weekly Reader Books

Weekly Reader Children's Book Club Presents

Two Good Friends

Pictures by Giulio Maestro

This book is a presentation of Newfield Publications,
Inc. Newfield Publications offers book clubs for children
from preschool through high school. For further
information write to: **Newfield Publications, Inc.**,
4343 Equity Drive, Columbus, Ohio 43228.

Published by arrangement with Judy Delton and
Giulio Maestro. Originally published by
Crown Publishers. Newfield Publications is a federally
registered trademark of Newfield Publications, Inc.
Weekly Reader is a federally registered trademark
of Weekly Reader Corporation.

Library of Congress Catalog Card Number: 73-88181
ISBN: 0-517-51401X
The text of this book is set in 18pt. Rector.
The illustrations are pencil drawings reproduced
in three colors.

Two Good Friends

Duck had cleaned his house.

All his floors were waxed.

All his furniture was polished.

He was admiring his clean rooms
when he heard a knock at the door.

It was Bear.

"Come in," said Duck, "but first wipe
your feet on the mat."

Bear wiped his feet on the mat
and went inside.

"Make yourself at home," said Duck.

"Thank you, I will," said Bear, and he
sat down in a shiny rocking chair.
Then he put his feet on Duck's table.

Duck reached for a newspaper and put
it under Bear's feet.

"What do you have to eat?" asked Bear.

"Nothing," said Duck.

"Nothing?" asked Bear.

"Today I cleaned my house," explained
  Duck. "I did not bake."

11

"Well, I have something," said Bear,
and he reached into his pocket and
took out two brownies.

"Bear," said Duck, "you are spilling
crumbs on my floor," and he reached
for another newspaper and put it
under Bear's chair.

Bear looked at the newspaper.

Then he looked at the two brownies.

"Duck," he said, "you are a very good housekeeper, but what good is a clean house if you have nothing to eat? Here, have a brownie."

Bear and Duck each ate a brownie and
spent the rest of the afternoon
putting a puzzle together.

The next day Duck went to visit Bear.
"Duck!" said Bear. "How nice to see
you. Come right in."

"M-m-m-m," said Duck. "What smells
so good?"

"I've been baking," said Bear, and he
pointed to two honey cakes and two
nut pies sitting on the table. "Brush
the flour off a chair and sit down."

"Bear," said Duck, "I can't sit down.
My feet are stuck."

"Oh dear," said Bear. "That's the
honey."

"Would you like honey cake or nut pie?"
he asked.

"Nut pie," said Duck, who had finally
managed to unstick his feet. "I've had
enough honey for one day."

"O.K.," said Bear, and he cut one piece of
nut pie for Duck and one for himself.

"May I have a plate?" asked Duck.

"The plates are dirty," said Bear.

"Well, then, may I have a fork?" asked
Duck.

"The forks are dirty too," said Bear.
He looked ashamed.

"Bear," said Duck, "how do you expect
me to eat?"

"I'm sorry," said Bear, "but today I
baked. I didn't clean the house or wash
the dishes. Maybe you can use your
wings. The pie will still taste good."

Duck and Bear each ate a piece of pie.
When Duck finished, he licked the tips
of his wings. "I must say, Bear, you
are a terrible housekeeper but your
nut pie is the best I have ever tasted."
Bear smiled. "Have another piece,"
he said.
"Gladly," said Duck, and they each ate
another piece.

The next day Bear went to Duck's house
with a surprise.
Duck was not at home but Bear went
inside anyway.

He put six raspberry muffins on the table and wrote a note. "From Bear," it said. Then he went home.

When Bear walked into his house, he was surprised. "I must be in the wrong house," he thought. His feet did not stick to the floor.

The dishes were washed and on the shelf.
He did not see his name where he had
written it in the flour on the table.

Instead he saw a note: "From Duck."

"I must thank Duck," thought Bear, but
   just then there was a knock on the
   door. It was Duck.
"Thank you for the muffins," said Duck.
"I was so surprised. And it's not even
   my birthday."

"And I have never seen my house so
  clean," said Bear. "I was surprised too."
"We really are good friends," said Duck.
"Yes!" cried Bear. "Let's celebrate!
  Come in and have some cookies."

"But first," added Bear, "wipe your feet
on the mat."

"Of course," said Duck. And he did.